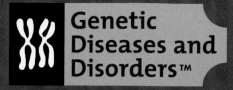

Genetic Diseases and Disorders™

Tay-Sachs Disease

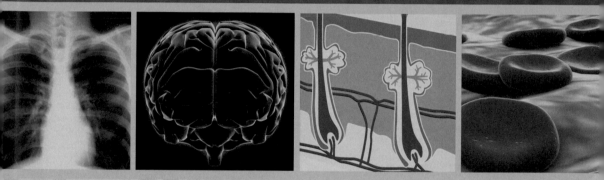

Julie Walker

The Rosen Publishing Group, Inc., New York

Published in 2007 by The Rosen Publishing Group, Inc.
29 East 21st Street, New York, NY 10010

Library of Congress Cataloging-in-Publication Data

Walker, Julie.
Tay-Sachs disease / Julie Walker.—1st ed.
    p. cm.—(Genetic diseases and disorders)
Includes bibliographical references and index.
ISBN 1-4042-0697-3 (library binding)
1. Tay-Sachs disease—Juvenile literature.
I. Title. II. Series.
RJ399.T36W35 2007
618.92'858845—dc22

                                                    2005031025

Printed in the United States of America

On the cover: Background: A computer-enhanced image of the human
brain. Foreground: A 3-D rendering of the human brain.

Contents

Introduction 4

1 What Is Tay-Sachs Disease? 6

2 Cause and Inheritance of Tay-Sachs Disease 13

3 Who Gets Tay-Sachs Disease? 22

4 Symptoms and Treatment of Tay-Sachs Disease 32

5 Screening and Prevention of Tay-Sachs Disease 43

Timeline 53

Glossary 55

For More Information 57

For Further Reading 59

Bibliography 60

Index 62

Introduction

A young couple leaves the hospital with a healthy baby boy. The weeks and months that follow are a blur of new experiences, sleepless nights, and firsts: first bottle, first bath, first giggle, and first solid food. The first few visits to the pediatrician come and go without a hitch. In every way, their baby appears to be healthy.

As the baby approaches the six-month mark, however, his parents notice a few subtle yet noteworthy changes in his development. There hasn't been anything major to write on the calendar for a while, not like the previous months when each day brought with it a new behavior milestone. He doesn't notice his favorite stuffed animal unless it's placed right in front of him. Yet, oddly enough, he seems to react strongly when the doorbell rings or the alarm clock buzzes in the morning.

At their next visit to the pediatrician, the parents ask the doctor about the changes they are noticing. Based on their observations, the doctor recommends that the baby undergo

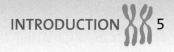

genetic testing. She explains that many people with genetic disorders do not exhibit symptoms immediately from birth. Because both parents are Jewish, the list of likely diagnoses narrows. Many genetic disorders are more common within specific cultural or ethnic groups. A simple blood test confirms their greatest fear: Tay-Sachs disease.

Tay-Sachs disease is fatal and currently has no cure. Most victims die before the age of five. Due to one inactive enzyme, the baby's central nervous system begins to shut down. He will begin to lose skills, one by one, just as his parents have noticed. By one year of age, he'll stop crawling, sitting, and reaching out for people and objects. As he grows older, he'll suffer from seizures, increasing loss of coordination, and the inability to swallow. In the final stages of the disease, he may become blind, mentally impaired, and paralyzed. For most families, caring for their child by themselves at home becomes impossible. They must either bring around-the-clock nursing services into their home or admit their child into a health care institution.

What Is Tay-Sachs Disease?

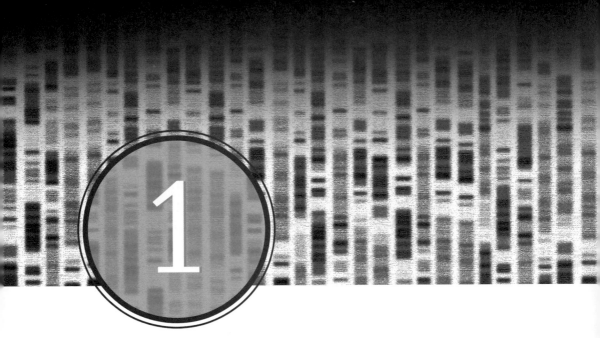

1

Tay-Sachs disease is a fatal genetic disorder. The most common form of the disease affects infants. People of eastern European Jewish descent are more likely to inherit Tay-Sachs disease than other populations. Currently, there are no effective treatments for Tay-Sachs disease, although screening and prevention programs are available for at-risk couples and for at-risk pregnant women.

The baby described in the introduction inherited Tay-Sachs disease from his parents. Half of his genes came from his mother, and the other half came from his father. Genes contain the code that the cells of the body need to make certain proteins called enzymes. If a gene is faulty, the body may not be able to produce a certain enzyme. If

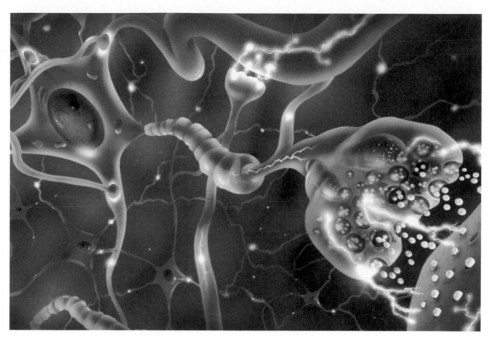

This illustration shows a type of cell called a neuron, the basic functional unit of the nervous system. The long extension of the neuron is called the axon and the other extensions are called dendrites. Neurons are responsible for sending messages from the body to the brain and back to the body again. Information is passed along as impulses jump from the axon of one neuron to the dendrites of another neuron.

an enzyme is absent, the body's cells cannot complete a specific job. In the case of Tay-Sachs disease, fatty substances cannot be broken down by the cell because an enzyme is missing. As a result, these fatty substances accumulate in the cells to a point where the cells can no longer function. Cells with high levels of fatty molecules, such as brain and nerve cells, are often affected. The death of these cells eventually results in the deterioration of the entire nervous system.

CGATTCTGAACATGATACGTACTGGTCCACTAGAACTGAACTCGAGAGGTACTAGA

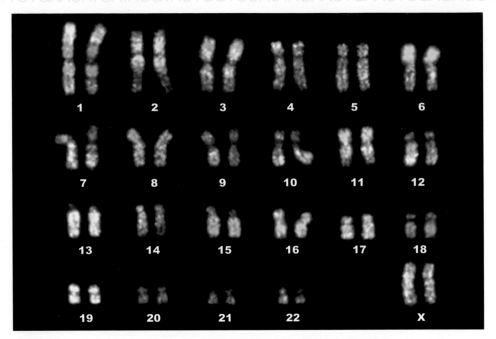

A karyotype shows the appearance and characteristics of every chromosome in one cell. The human karyotype pictured above shows all forty-six chromosomes, organized into twenty-three matching pairs. The twenty-third pair, seen in the bottom right corner, is a set of X chromosomes, indicating that this is a female karyotype. A karyotype is a useful tool to help geneticists diagnose genetic abnormalities in their patients.

What Is a Genetic Disorder?

Genetic disorders are passed from parents to their children. Deep within each cell of the body is a structure called the nucleus, which contains deoxyribonucleic acid, or DNA. DNA contains the genetic information that determines how an organic life-form will grow and develop. It also contains the master code for running the daily operations of our cells and determines which genetic traits, such as eye color, will be passed from a parent to his or her child.

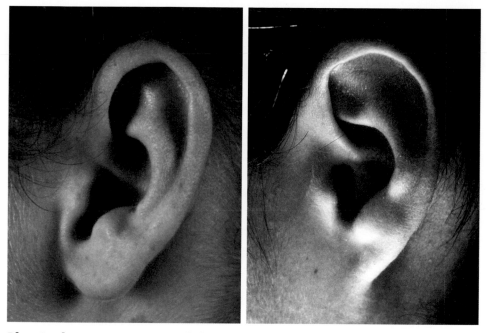

Physical traits are passed from parents to their offspring. Genes from the mother and father combine to create the individual traits of their child. One easily observable trait is the shape of the earlobe. The gene controlling the free-hanging earlobe *(left)* is dominant over the gene responsible for the attached earlobe *(right)*. For a baby to be born with attached earlobes, he or she must have received two recessive genes, one from each parent.

Chromosomes are bundles of DNA held together with proteins. Each cell of the human body contains twenty-three pairs of rod-shaped chromosomes. The origin of these chromosomes is simple: twenty-three single chromosomes come from the mother, and twenty-three single chromosomes come from the father. Each chromosome can contain up to thousands of smaller units, called genes, and each gene contains a unique code for making one or more proteins. Proteins are molecules that not only form cells but also help cells to function

ATCGATTCTGAACATGATACGTACTGGTCCACTAGAACTGAACTCGAGAGGTACTAG

THE DISCOVERY OF TAY-SACHS

In April 1881, a British ophthalmologist named Dr. Warren Tay (1843–1927) described the case of a twelve-month-old patient with unusual symptoms to the Ophthalmological Society of the United Kingdom. Dr. Tay noticed a bright red spot on the retina of his patient's eye. The boy also had trouble simply holding up his head and moving his arms and legs, which was unusual for a child at his stage of development. The boy died at twenty months of age. Later, Dr. Tay observed similar symptoms in two of the boy's siblings.

Just six years later, in 1887, a neurologist from New York named Dr. Bernard Sachs (1858–1944) observed changes inside the cells of a patient with similar symptoms to those shown by Dr. Tay's patient. At the time, Dr. Sachs was unaware of Dr. Tay's findings.

Over a span of two decades, Dr. Sachs treated eight children, all with the same damage to the retina of their eyes and the same deterioration of their nerve cells. In a 1910 article in the *Journal of Experimental Medicine*, he reported that these

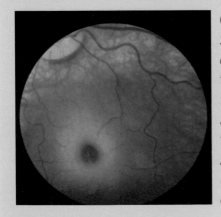

One of the earliest signs of Tay-Sachs disease in infants is the cherry-red spot on the retina of the eye. The retina is a membrane in the back of the eye that receives an image from the lens and sends it to the brain through the optic nerve. As Tay-Sachs progresses, the nerve cells in the retina may be damaged enough to result in blindness.

patients suffered from a "balloon-like swelling of the dendrites." (A dendrite is a structure in a neuron, or nerve cell.) Dr. Sachs was also a psychologist, and he spent long hours at the bedside of his patients, meticulously observing and recording their symptoms and behavior. Dr. Sachs also began to notice that the disease seemed to appear only in children of families who were of Jewish descent.

By 1896, a number of other physicians had observed and reported similar symptoms in their young patients. Scientists named the disease after the two men who identified it: Tay-Sachs disease.

properly. If the genetic code for one gene is altered even slightly, the protein it is responsible for making may not be produced or may be produced abnormally. As a result, all the cells in the body that rely on that protein will be affected.

Mutations

Mutations are changes in the genetic code that may result in disease. Let's say a mutation occurs randomly in one individual. The mutated gene may be passed to that person's offspring. The more children that person has, the more likely the mutated gene is to propagate, or continue, through future generations. If that person has no children, the mutation ends with him or her.

Since chromosomes occur in pairs, and genes are contained within chromosomes, genes also occur in pairs. Most genetic disorders require that both genes in a pair be mutated for the symptoms of the disease to be expressed

CGATTCTGAACATGATACGTACTGGTCCACTAGAACTGAACTCGAGAGGTACTAGAC

in the individual. This is known as an autosomal recessive genetic disorder. Tay-Sachs disease, along with hundreds of others, falls into this category. If a person possesses one normal gene and one mutated gene, he or she is referred to as a carrier. The healthy gene overpowers the mutated gene, so the carrier does not suffer from the disorder. Tay-Sachs disease is inherited through two carrier parents. Each parent has to contribute one mutated gene to the child to provide the child with the recessive pair required to produce the disease.

Some Variations of the Disease

Infantile Tay-Sachs, the most common form of Tay-Sachs disease, is generally diagnosed in the first four to eight months of an infant's life. Infantile Tay-Sachs disease is always fatal, and children affected by it usually die between the ages of three and five years.

Another form of Tay-Sachs disease is known as adult-onset or late-onset Tay-Sachs disease (LOTS). The symptoms of LOTS are considerably milder than those of infantile Tay-Sachs disease, and LOTS is usually diagnosed around the time the patient is twenty years old. Unlike infantile Tay-Sachs disease, LOTS rarely lowers the life expectancy of its victims.

Cause and Inheritance
of Tay-Sachs Disease

2

Tay-Sachs disease falls into a category of rare genetic disorders known as lysosomal storage diseases. Lysosomes are one type of the many small structures, called organelles, found inside most animal cells. Each lysome is responsible for disposing waste materials that the cell no longer needs. Lysosomal storage diseases impair the ability of a cell to dispose of its waste products. If a cell cannot dispose of its waste products, the waste will begin to accumulate in the cell.

Waste products of a cell may include fat molecules (lipids), protein molecules, or carbohydrate molecules. When a cell is finished with any of these substances, enzymes break the molecule down into simpler, smaller units so it can be disposed of.

CGATTCTGAACATGATACGTACTGGTCCACTAGAACTGAACTCGAGAGGTACTAGAC

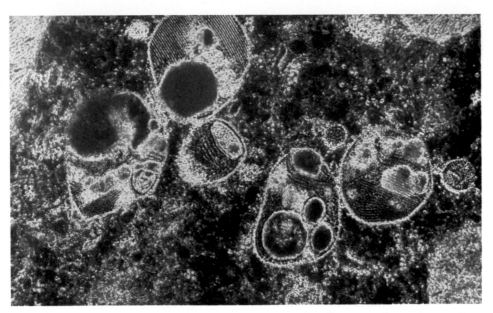

This photograph of lysosomes in an animal cell was taken through the lens of an electron microscope. The tiny organelles have been magnified 12,500 times their actual size. Lysosomes contain enzymes responsible for breaking down all types of food molecules.

Enzymes and Lysosomes

Enzymes are the proteins that jump-start all of the chemical reactions in your body's cells. In fact, thousands of different enzymes are at work in your body right now. Enzymes are made of smaller particles known as amino acids. Twenty unique amino acids combine in thousands of ways to create all the enzymes required to keep the human body in healthy, working order. Because each amino acid is a different shape, every enzyme is a different shape. The success of an enzyme within a cell is dependent upon its shape.

Enzymes are found inside lysosomes, where they are constantly at work. The shape of each enzyme is designed to "fit" together with the shape of one specific type of waste product. The enzyme and the waste molecule lock together much like puzzle pieces. As soon as the two become linked, the enzyme begins to do its job. It initiates a chemical reaction which begins to break down the waste product. Upon completion of the chemical reaction, the new substances may either be reused by the cell or disposed of completely. An enzyme built incorrectly, meaning that it has the wrong shape, will not be able to do its job effectively.

The production of enzymes is controlled by genes. Although rare, a gene may occasionally be the victim of a random mutation. A mutated gene may cause the cell to produce a defective enzyme, or the cell might not produce the enzyme at all.

Enzymes active within the lysosomes are categorized as degradative enzymes. This title is fitting because to degrade means to dispose of, and enzymes dispose of waste. If one type of degradative enzyme is missing or damaged as a result of a mutation, the waste it usually disposes of will begin to accumulate in the lysosomes. As waste products build up in the lysosomes, the cell itself will begin to deteriorate, or break down. These damaged cells eventually begin to affect tissues, organs, organ systems, and the organism as a whole.

There are many different lysosomal storage diseases, each resulting from a missing or malfunctioning enzyme. The type of waste that accumulates, and the location in the body where the accumulation is the greatest, varies for each different lysosomal storage disease. These factors are responsible for creating the variety of symptoms that appear in the victims of lysosomal storage diseases. In addition to Tay-Sachs disease, other lysosomal storage diseases that have been identified

TCGATTCTGAACATGATACGTACTGGTCCACTAGAACTGAACTCGAGAGGTACTAGA

Computer graphics are often helpful to illustrate complex chemical reactions that take place inside cells. Here, enzymes (colored
red, pink, green, and blue) bind with yellow substrate molecules.
The enzyme and the substrate fit together like a lock and key.
Once attached, the enzyme begins to chemically break down the
substrate into smaller, simpler molecules.

include Gaucher disease, Niemann-Pick disease, Sandhoff
disease, Sly syndrome, and Canavan disease. Within the
past twenty years, scientists have discovered a unique disease for almost every lysosomal enzyme.

The Hex-A Enzyme

The name of the enzyme that is abnormal in Tay-Sachs disease
is called Beta-hexosaminidase-A, or hex-A. The specific function

of hex-A in the cells of the body is to break down a lipid called GM2 ganglioside. This fatty substance is present primarily in nerve cells in the brain. GM2 ganglioside is not related to the type of fats that you eat, but instead is a normal component of the cell membrane. The cell membrane is the outermost layer of all types of animal cells, including nerve cells. Periodically, the cell membrane gets worn out and its component parts need to be broken down and replaced.

In Tay-Sachs victims, the hex-A enzyme is produced in extremely small quantities, if at all. This critical discovery was made in 1969, by Dr. Shintaro Okada and Dr. John O'Brien, who were working at the University of California, San Diego. It was not until this discovery was made that scientists could develop a method of screening individuals in order to identify parents at risk of having children with this devastating disorder.

When the hex-A enzyme is missing completely, the lysosomes cannot function properly. GM2 ganglioside is not broken down, and it gradually begins to accumulate in the lysosomes. The lysosomes swell in size and continue to do so until they fill the entire nerve cell. This swelling eventually leads to the death of the cell.

Out of all the organs in the body, the brain contains the highest concentration of GM2 ganglioside. As more and more nerve cells in the brain die, the brain slowly loses its ability to function. Unfortunately, brain cells replenish at an extremely slow rate. In the final stages of Tay-Sachs disease, so much of the brain has been destroyed that the patient begins to lose vital life functions, such as the ability to control breathing or heart rate.

Based on the chemicals involved in the disease, scientists sometimes refer to Tay-Sachs disease by two other names: GM2 gangliosidosis or hexosaminidase A deficiency.

CGATTCTGAACATGATACGTACTGGTCCACTAGAACTGAACTCGAGAGGTACTAGAG

PUNNETT SQUARE

The chart below, known as a Punnett square, illustrates the probability that two Tay-Sachs carriers will produce a child with the disease.

H = Dominant Tay-Sachs   h = Recessive Tay-Sachs
        disease gene   disease gene

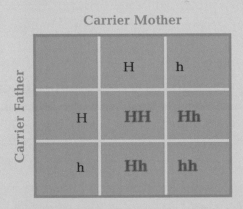

Carrier Mother

The possible outcomes for the gene pairs of the offspring are:

25 percent HH = pure dominant (two healthy genes)
50 percent Hh = heterozygous (carrier)
25 percent hh = pure recessive (child with Tay-Sachs disease)

In the case where only one parent is a carrier for Tay-Sachs disease, there is no possible way that a baby with the disorder could be produced. There will be, however, a 50 percent chance that his or her offspring will be carriers. This occurrence is illustrated in the Punnett square on the next page.

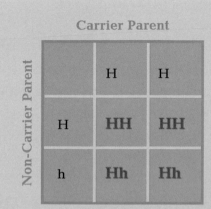

	Carrier Parent	
	H	H
H	HH	HH
h	Hh	Hh

Non-Carrier Parent

The possible outcomes for the gene pairs of the offspring are:

50 percent HH = pure dominant (two healthy genes)
50 percent Hh = heterozygous (carrier)

Creating Punnett squares for autosomal recessive disorders such as Tay-Sachs disease helps to show how quickly a mutated gene can invade a population. Only one parent needs to be a carrier of the Tay-Sachs gene in order to produce many more carrier children. Clearly, as the number of Tay-Sachs carriers increases in a population, the number of affected offspring increases as well.

How Is Tay-Sachs Inherited?

Tay-Sachs disease is one of many genetic disorders classified as an autosomal recessive disorder. Out of the twenty-three different pairs of chromosomes a human possesses, autosomes are any of the pairs other than the sex chromosomes. (The sex chromosomes are the twenty-third pair.) The gene that is responsible for making the enzyme hex-A is located on chromosome 15. When the hex-A gene is changed, or mutated, the enzyme is either not produced at all or is produced in very small quantities.

An autosomal recessive disorder is passed from parents to offspring through genes. Both parents must carry the mutated

TCGATTCTGAACATGATACGTACTGGTCCACTAGAACTGAACTCGAGAGGTACTAGA

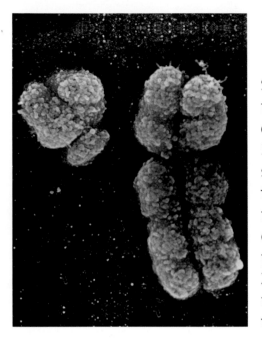

Seen through an electron microscope, these human sex chromosomes are magnified 35,000 times. On the left is the smaller Y chromosome, and on the right is the larger X chromosome. Females inherit two X chromosomes, one from each parent, while males inherit an X chromosome from the mother and a Y chromosome from the father.

gene—one copy is not strong enough to produce the disease. An individual with one healthy gene and one mutated Tay-Sachs gene will not develop the disorder. His or her dominant copy of the gene will outweigh the recessive gene, and his or her cells will successfully produce adequate amounts of the hex-A enzyme. Instead, he or she will be a carrier for the disorder, meaning that he or she could potentially pass Tay-Sachs on to his or her offspring.

When fertilization occurs, each parent passes on one of the genes in a pair to the offspring. The female provides an egg cell, and the male provides the sperm cell. These special cells, called gametes, possess half the number of chromosomes of any other cell in the human body. Each egg cell produced by a carrier mother, for instance, has a 50 percent chance of containing the healthy gene. The same is true for each of the sperm cells produced by a carrier father.

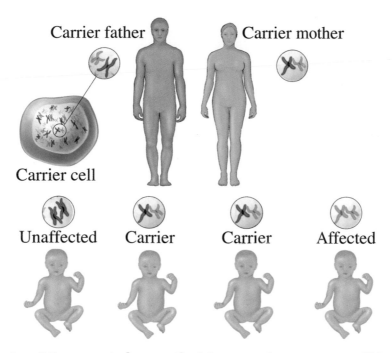

Carrier father   Carrier mother

Carrier cell

Unaffected   Carrier   Carrier   Affected

There is a 25 percent chance that two carrier parents will have a baby with Tay-Sachs disease. There is a 50 percent chance that the child will be a carrier. Visualizing such devastating odds stresses the importance of carrier screening tests. Scientific discoveries, combined with progressive educational programs, have led to a major decline in the occurrence of Tay-Sachs disease.

In order for Tay-Sachs disease to be transmitted to a child, both parents must be carriers of the disorder. They each must pass a copy of the inactive gene on chromosome 15 to their baby. The physical symptoms of Tay-Sachs disease can only appear when the child receives two mutated copies of the gene, one from each parent. Couples that are both carriers have a 25 percent chance of producing a baby with Tay-Sachs disease. In addition, carrier couples have a 50 percent chance of producing children that are carriers for the disorder.

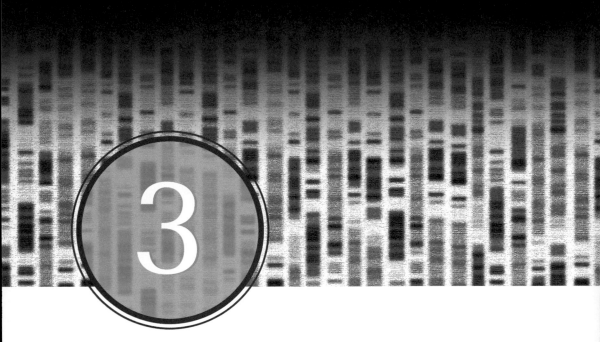

Occasionally, genetic disorders are more prevalent within specific cultural and ethnic groups. This is definitely the case for Tay-Sachs disease. Approximately 85 percent of children born today with infantile Tay-Sachs disease are of Jewish descent. In the United States, approximately 1 out of every 27 people of Jewish heritage is a carrier for the disorder. For the general U.S. population, the statistic drops to 1 in every 250 people.

Within the broad category of the Jewish population, three distinct subgroups exist. The first group, Ashkenazi Jews, originate from western, eastern, and central Europe, especially from the countries of Germany, Poland, Romania, and Russia. The second group,

Sephardic Jews, derive from Mediterranean regions, specifically from Spain and the North African countries of Libya and Morocco. The final group consists of Mizrachi Jews, stemming primarily from the Middle Eastern countries of Iran and Iraq.

Of these three geographically distinct groups, people descending from the Ashkenazis have the greatest risk for carrying the mutation for Tay-Sachs disease. One reason may simply be in the numbers: 80 percent of Jews worldwide attribute their origins to this eastern European group, and most Jewish people in the United States can trace their origins to the Ashkenazim. Historically, Ashkenazi Jews immigrated to the United States in the greatest numbers between 1880 and 1920. In 1880, 250,000 Ashkenazi Jews were residing in the United States. By 1920, this number had jumped to 3.5 million.

Prior to the carrier screening and education programs that began in the 1970s, infantile Tay-Sachs disease was about 100 times more common among Ashkenazi Jews than any other ethnic group. In the United States, 1 out of every 3,600 births among couples of Ashkenazi descent resulted in a baby with Tay-Sachs disease. Thanks to widespread screening programs, Tay Sachs disease is virtually nonexistent among Ashkenazi Jews today. This does not mean that the Tay-Sachs gene is nonexistent in other populations, however. For example, scientists have reported a higher than average number of Tay-Sachs carriers in non-Jewish French Canadians living near the Saint Lawrence River, in the Cajun community of Louisiana, and within Irish populations in the United States.

Why would people of Jewish heritage be so much more susceptible to a disease than any other group? To answer this question, we must explore their cultural history. Where were they located? Did they migrate or stay in one geographic location? How did the people live? Answering some of these

CGATTCTGAACATGATACGTACTGGTCCACTAGAACTGAACTCGAGAGGTACTAGAC

This marble sarcophagus, dating back to between the first and third centuries AD, is decorated with an image of the exodus of the Jews. It currently resides in the Archaeological Museum of Split, Croatia. This detailed scene depicts one of the many forced migrations of the Jewish people.

questions will help us understand why Tay-Sachs disease is more prevalent among people of Jewish descent.

An Insular Population

To start at the beginning, we need to go back to a man named Abraham, who lived in ancient Israel. Traditionally, Jews have viewed Abraham as their common ancestor. Most Jews today attribute their origins to one ethnic group descended from Abraham.

Over the course of history, however, people of Jewish heritage were forced to migrate away from present-day Israel. In 586 BC, the kingdom of Judah was conquered by the Babylonians. The Babylonians destroyed the temple in Jerusalem, which was the center of Jewish worship, and forced the Jews out of their homeland. These extensive migrations, which came to be known as the Diaspora, resulted in the formation of the three subgroups discussed earlier.

Despite being uprooted and forced to move great distances, most Jewish communities remained intact. Their beliefs held them together during times of persecution. Well into the nineteenth century, many Jews continued to live primarily among themselves and marry within their own communities.

Populations consisting of one ethnic or cultural group of people are sometimes referred to as being insular, or focused on their own community and way of life. There are

TCGATTCTGAACATGATACGTACTGGTCCACTAGAACTGAACTCGAGAGGTACTAG

many reasons why a group of people such as the Jews might become insular over the course of hundreds of years. Jewish religious beliefs differed from those of the people around them, and the Jews often ended up being unfairly persecuted.

After the massive migrations from Israel to the surrounding regions, Jewish communities began experiencing some negative effects of their insularity. Politicians and religious leaders passed laws regarding where and how Jewish immigrants should live in their countries. Many Jews were forced to live in restricted urban areas called ghettos. In some countries, Jewish people were not allowed to interact with the native population in any way. Whether through their own free will or not, people of Jewish heritage remained insular for hundreds of years.

A Smaller Gene Pool

A gene pool consists of all the genes passed from one generation to another in a segment of the population. The smaller the population of breeding adults, the smaller the gene pool will be. As soon as a gene enters the group, it can be passed down through the generations.

The smaller the population is, the more likely the gene will remain in the group for a long period of time. Ethnically insular communities often have a higher susceptibility to genetic diseases than ethnically diverse communities.

When an individual carries a mutated copy of the Tay-Sachs gene, it is very likely that he or she will pass it on to his or her offspring. Once such a gene enters an insular population, it is confined to that community. The gene will

A photograph taken around 1905 depicts a Jewish ghetto in New York City. Just as in European ghettos, tenement buildings were often crowded, unsanitary breeding grounds for diseases such as tuberculosis. Medical services were often too expensive for impoverished citizens to afford.

naturally remain within the population for as long as it remains insular.

A Dangerous Trade-Off

Historically, it is difficult to know exactly when the gene for Tay-Sachs entered the Jewish community. From about the thirteenth to nineteenth centuries, Jewish families were forced to live primarily in urban ghettos and had no access to sophisticated medicine. Many families experienced a high infant mortality rate, and it was not unusual for children to die before the age of three. The disease was likely in existence long before doctors were able to recognize its symptoms and diagnose it.

Contagious diseases were a greater threat to families living in the close quarters of a populated ghetto. One such epidemic that spread through most European cities as early as the seventeenth century was tuberculosis. Tuberculosis is an infectious bacterial disease that affects the lungs and is easily spread through the air.

Because tuberculosis is so contagious, it spread quickly in highly populated areas. The bacterial disease ravaged the ghettos. Those fortunate individuals who escaped infection were able to pass their genes to their offspring. Some data exists which indicates that members of the Jewish ghettos were more likely to survive tuberculosis than non-Jewish urban residents. Although the data is inconclusive, some scientists believe that it was more than luck that allowed for lower mortality rates within these Jewish communities.

Tay-Sachs Takes Root

Individuals possessing one copy of the gene for Tay-Sachs disease appeared to be less susceptible to tuberculosis. Carriers of the mutated gene seemed to be healthier than noncarriers. As an increasing number of carriers survived tuberculosis, the Tay-Sachs gene became more established in the Jewish communities. Over the course of many generations, Tay-Sachs carriers began to marry and have children. Remember, when two carrier parents have a child, there is a 50 percent chance that the child will also be a carrier. Healthy carrier parents were producing many healthy descendants. Also recall, however, that the same parents

Due to the discovery of effective antibiotics to treat tuberculosis in the late 1940s, the death toll from this devastating bacterial disease dropped dramatically during the next decade in the United States. This photograph shows people signing up for chest X-rays at a mobile clinic in Los Angeles, California, in 1957. Public awareness and early detection programs helped to stop the spread of the disease.

CGATTCTGAACATGATACGTACTGGTCCACTAGAACTGAACTCGAGAGGTACTAGA

Much like Tay-Sachs, sickle-cell anemia is a genetic disease specific to a certain population. People of African ancestry are much more susceptible to this hereditary blood disease than members of any other cultural group. On the far left is an abnormal red blood cell in the shape of a sickle. Next to it is a round, healthy, disk-shaped red blood cell. As the body forms more and more of the sickle-shaped blood cells, a potentially fatal condition results.

have a 25 percent chance of producing a baby with two copies of the mutated gene. Over time, Tay-Sachs disease emerged as an increasing number of babies were born possessing two copies of the mutated gene, one from each carrier parent. Some researchers believe that Tay-Sachs carriers may be more resistant to tuberculosis. However, this theory is still very controversial, and more research needs to be done to determine if this is true.

The Founder Effect

When a small number of people establish a new population, they are known as founders. A founder who develops a mutation in a gene may pass it on to his or her offspring. The more insular a population is, the more likely it is that the mutation will be inherited by many individuals. Clearly, the more offspring the original founder has, the more likely the faulty genes will become fixed in the population. If the founder does not reproduce, the mutation ends with him or her.

In a less insular population, people marry outside of their culture, ethnicity, religion, or social class. This practice naturally leads to a larger gene pool, thereby diffusing the effects of any mutations that enter.

4

Tay-Sachs disease is most common in infants, and deterioration of the nerve cells begins before the baby is born. Any observable symptoms, however, do not appear for several months. The first signs of Tay-Sachs vary, and they are noticeable at different ages in different children. Initial symptoms usually begin to appear around six months of age. Parents may notice that the baby's development slows and peripheral vision weakens, and the baby startles easily. Upon careful examination of the eyes, a doctor may report a red spot on the baby's retina.

By one year of age, the infant begins losing motor skills. The baby stops crawling, turning over, sitting, and reaching out to objects and people. Because of the brain's slow deterioration, symptoms begin to worsen in the months and years that follow. The infant begins experiencing seizures that require constant medication. Difficulty swallowing develops into the complete inability to eat, requiring the use of a feeding tube. Weakened vision worsens to the point of complete blindness. Progressive loss of brain development leads to mental impairment. In the final stages of the disease, paralysis sets in.

Children with Tay-Sachs disease lead tragically brief lives, seldom living past the age of five. Their brains become so badly ravaged that even the simplest life functions, such as breathing and maintaining a heart rate, are compromised. The child's seizures will become so severe that they will not be able to be controlled with drugs and medication. Most families find that they can no longer care for their sick child in their own home. Eventually, every system in the child's body becomes damaged in some way, including the immune system. Even the most common infection becomes impossible for the child to fend off. Often, the actual cause of death in Tay-Sachs patients is attributed to an infection such as pneumonia.

Symptoms of Adult/Late-Onset Tay-Sachs

Much less common than its infantile counterpart, late-onset Tay-Sachs disease, or LOTS, is usually not diagnosed until adolescence. People with LOTS do produce the hex-A enzyme, but the amount produced is only about 10 to 15 percent of that produced in a healthy individual. It is not enough hex-A to prevent buildup of the GM2 ganglioside in the nerve cells of the brain.

Initial symptoms of LOTS are usually quite mild and may include light tremors or twitching, poor coordination, weakness or cramping of the muscles, and nasal or slurred speech. The lack of any severely debilitating symptoms has resulted in many patients being misdiagnosed. Because the muscular symptoms of LOTS are of a mild nature, many doctors have been led to believe that these patients might be experiencing the beginning stages of other diseases such as multiple sclerosis or muscular dystrophy. A test analyzing the amount of hex-A enzyme in a patient's blood or the mutations in a patient's DNA is needed to determine if he or she is afflicted with LOTS.

As time progresses, so do the symptoms of LOTS. Patients may experience ataxia, or the inability to coordinate voluntary muscle movements. This, along with general muscle weakness, may result in difficulty climbing stairs and walking steadily. Some patients develop mild intellectual impairments such as loss of memory comprehension and reduced attention span. Forty percent of LOTS patients report suffering from psychiatric symptoms, such as depression. Fortunately, with the support of various health services and medications, LOTS patients are usually able to manage their symptoms and live long and productive lives.

Treatment and Current Research

At this time, there is no cure for either infantile or late-onset Tay-Sachs disease. Treatment involves dealing with the symptoms as they arise. For example, when a baby with Tay-Sachs develops seizures, the baby is treated with antiepileptic medications. The seizures cannot be stopped, but they can be managed.

The good news is that there have been many hopeful discoveries involving potential cures for Tay-Sachs and other lysosomal storage disorders. The National Tay-Sachs and Allied Diseases Association (NTSAD) has examined six therapeutic approaches for treating the disease.

Enzyme Replacement Therapy

Enzyme replacement therapy, or ERT, attempts to do just what its name implies. If a missing or defective enzyme (such as hex-A) could somehow be replaced in the cells with a functional enzyme, all lysosomal storage diseases would be cured. Unfortunately, what sounds good in theory does not always work in practice. While ERT has been successful for treating some diseases, it has not proven to be effective for the treatment of Tay-Sachs disease. Because Tay-Sachs is a neurological disorder, meaning that it affects the brain, the replacement enzyme must be able to travel to the brain from the bloodstream. Enzymes are very large protein molecules, and they are blocked from doing this by what is known as

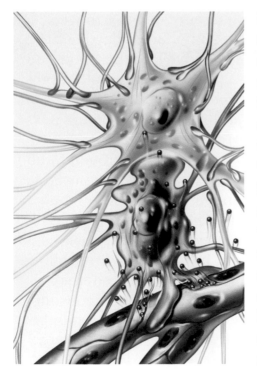

If scientists could create a drug or therapy to treat Tay-Sachs disease, it might follow this route to the nervous system. At the bottom, a small blood vessel, or capillary, carries molecules throughout the bloodstream. When the blood reaches the brain, only the tiniest molecules can pass through the outermost membrane of the capillary and move on into the nerve cells. Finding a route for the enzymes through the blood-brain barrier may result in a cure for Tay-Sachs and many other devastating diseases.

ATCGATTCTGAACATGATACGTACTGGTCCACTAGAACTGAACTCGAGAGGTACTAG

the blood-brain barrier. The job of the blood-brain barrier is to protect the brain from harmful substances in the bloodstream. It protects the brain so well that it will not allow enzymes to cross the barrier, making ERT ineffective in treating lysosomal storage diseases that affect the central nervous system.

Bone Marrow Transplantation

Most cells found in the brain are incapable of dividing and multiplying like other body cells. So where do new brain cells come from? Many derive either from bone marrow or from neural stem cells within the brain.

Stem cells are immature cells that are capable of developing into all of the different types of cells in the body. Stem cell research is a new and promising realm of medicine that will hopefully lead to cures for the most devastating diseases. Scientists believe that introducing either bone marrow cells or neural stem cells into a patient with Tay-Sachs may lead to a cure. The cells should, theoretically, move into the brain and begin to multiply. These new, healthy cells would begin producing the necessary hex-A enzyme.

Like ERT, many obstacles stand in the way of such a seemingly simple idea. Bone marrow transplants have been attempted in Tay-Sachs patients, but they have proven to be ineffective. A bone marrow transplant is a procedure used to transplant healthy bone marrow into a patient whose bone marrow is not functioning properly. The process was able to slow the destruction of the central nervous system but was not able to stop it completely. Although bone marrow transplants can have beneficial effects, they are difficult procedures. Finding a matching donor is very difficult and time consuming, the surgical procedure involved is risky, and the number of healthy cells introduced into the patient may not be large enough to make a difference.

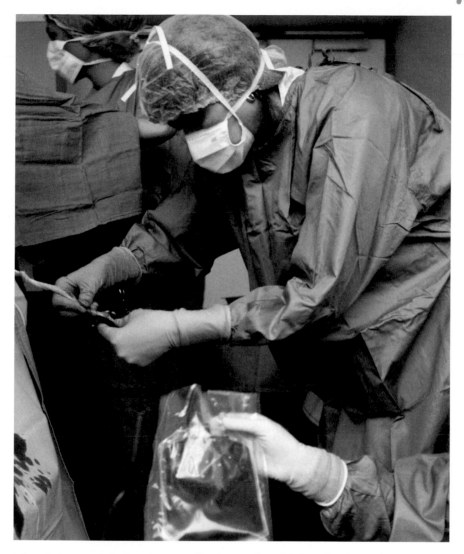

Physicians obtain stem cells from fetal blood taken from a baby's umbilical cord. Parents may choose to keep their baby's fetal cord blood for future use. The blood is frozen and stored in extremely cold tanks of liquid nitrogen. The stem cells may be harvested later if the child develops any number of fatal blood diseases. The parents may also choose to donate the blood for use in scientific research projects. Experimenting with stem cells may some day lead to a cure for Tay-Sachs disease.

ATCGATTCTGAACATGATACGTACTGGTCCACTAGAACTGAACTCGAGAGGTACTAG

Neural Stem Cell Therapy

Research in the area of neural stem cell therapy is new, and it may hold more promise than its bone marrow counterpart. Rather than finding a living donor, frozen fetal cord blood, or blood taken from the umbilical cord and placenta when a baby is born, may be used to obtain stem cells. Stem cells may be able to be genetically altered to produce and secrete greater amounts of the hex-A enzyme.

Although clinical trials involving human stem cells may not happen for many years, scientists have already begun experimenting with mice. Scientists are beginning to observe beneficial effects of stem cell therapy within the brains of mice with Tay-Sachs disease. Neural stem cell therapy may someday provide a cure for lysosomal storage diseases affecting the brain.

Gene Therapy

Gene therapy is another new and exciting area of research for Tay-Sachs patients. In the simplest terms, gene therapy involves taking a normal gene and transferring it into cells with an abnormal gene. By artificially adding large numbers of the active gene, scientists hypothesize that the cells will be able to compensate for their hex-A deficiency and break down an adequate amount of GM2 ganglioside. If the active gene can "take over" the abnormal genes, further destruction of the nervous system can be prevented.

The most common method of introducing new genes into the body is by using something known as a viral vector. A virus is a tiny particle that typically infects and destroys cells, causing disease. A viral vector is a virus that has been engineered in a laboratory so that it cannot cause disease. Since it has been rendered harmless, a viral vector may serve as a messenger to carry the active gene to the cells in any of the body's organs.

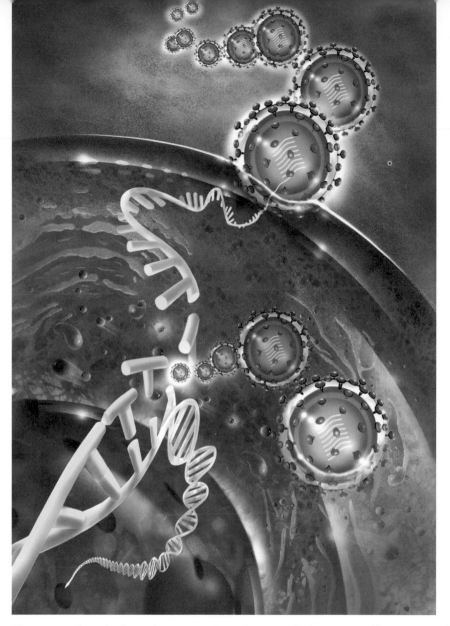

The use of a viral vector may one day result in a cure for Tay-Sachs disease. Scientists consider viruses to be nonliving, yet they contain genetic material and they are capable of reproducing. However, viruses cannot reproduce on their own. They require a living cell, called a host. This illustration shows the spherical influenza, or flu, virus infecting a host cell. Some of the virus's genetic material conceals itself within the host's DNA. In this way, the virus uses the host cell to mass-produce copies of itself.

TCGATTCTGAACATGATACGTACTGGTCCACTAGAACTGAACTCGAGAGGTACTAGA

A scientist works with viral vectors underneath a sterile hood. Not only do researchers need to protect themselves when handling potentially harmful materials, but the experiments also need protection. Manipulating living cells in the laboratory requires meticulous conditions and constant care. The slightest contamination can ruin weeks or months of hard work in the lab.

While scientists have high expectations for the use of gene therapy in finding a cure for lysosomal storage diseases like Tay-Sachs, they cannot ignore the many limitations that exist. The science behind creating virus vectors and inserting them into the body is still in the early stages of development. Scientists agree that making a viral vector is difficult, particularly for brain cells. Geneticists must also find a way to keep the newly introduced genes from becoming active in cells that are not located in the central nervous system where they are not needed. Scientists do not know if they will be able to introduce the active genes in great enough numbers to make a physical difference in the health of the patient. A final trial facing gene and stem cell therapy involves politics. Both forms of therapy have ignited great debates over the ethical and moral nature of the procedures involved. Is a stem cell considered a living being? Should humans be tampering with genes? As long as these questions are being debated by lawmakers, the future of any human trials is unknown. Most major scientific research projects in the

United States are funded, at least in part, by the federal government. The National Institutes of Health (NIH) enforces a strict set of guidelines regarding projects that involve stem cell and gene therapy. Research projects may not even begin until protocols and procedures pass extensive review processes outlined by the NIH.

Substrate Deprivation Therapy

One area of current research that is already making a difference in the lives of patients with certain lysosomal storage diseases is substrate deprivation therapy. A substrate is a molecule that is changed or broken down by an enzyme. In the case of Tay-Sachs disease, the substrate is GM2 ganglioside. The job of the hex-A enzyme is to break down GM2 ganglioside into smaller molecules that the cell can digest. When hex-A is absent or deficient, the substrate accumulates to dangerous levels. Using substrate deprivation therapy, special chemicals called inhibitors will stop GM2 ganglioside from being made, or synthesized by the cell.

For each lysosomal storage disease, the accumulating substrate is different. So far, substrate deprivation therapy has been tested and used successfully only with patients suffering from lysosomal storage disorders that do not involve the nervous system. One example is Gaucher disease, which affects cells in the bone marrow, spleen, and liver.

Metabolic Bypass Therapy

Metabolic bypass therapy is a treatment for lysosomal storage diseases that is still largely theoretical. Metabolic bypass therapy is a biochemical process that attempts to bypass, or find a way around, the cells' need for the inactive enzyme. If the cells of a Tay-Sachs patient could find some other means of degrading the GM2 ganglioside, the cells would have no need for the hex-A enzyme.

TCGATTCTGAACATGATACGTACTGGTCCACTAGAACTGAACTCGAGAGGTACTAG

A child with Tay-Sachs disease undergoes physical therapy in a swimming pool. Aquatic exercises and therapy can help increase muscle strength and improve balance and coordination. While there is still no cure for Tay-Sachs disease, treatments such as physical therapy can help to ease the symptoms of the disorder.

Metabolic bypass therapy aims to introduce special chemicals called activators (the opposite of inhibitors) into the cells. Activators increase the ability of other enzymes to break down larger amounts of the GM2 ganglioside. Bypassing the need for hex-A, the cells will be able to break down sufficient amounts of the lipid and will maintain a healthy status.

As with all of the other approaches to treating Tay-Sachs disease discussed already, this approach is much easier said than done. Metabolic bypass therapy is still just a theory. Scientists all over the world are working on cures for lysosomal storage diseases. What is only a theory today may one day become a cure for Tay-Sachs disease.

Screening and Prevention of Tay-Sachs Disease

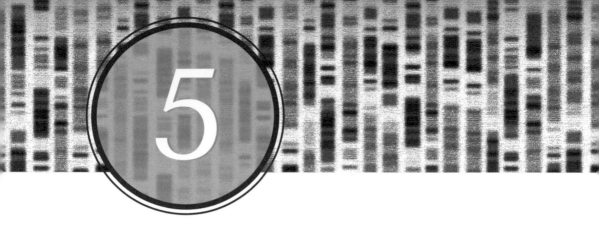

5

Shortly after the discovery that the hex-A enzyme was the missing link in Tay-Sachs patients, medical professionals began an intensive, widespread campaign to educate and screen all adults of Jewish descent. Beginning in the early 1970s, carrier couples could be identified and warned of their potential risk of having a baby with Tay-Sachs disease. These at-risk couples could then use the information gleaned from the screening to explore options that would spare their families the tragedy of Tay-Sachs.

The diagnosis of a carrier means that the carrier's relatives may also be carriers of the Tay-Sachs gene. Any individual who is diagnosed as being a carrier for Tay-Sachs disease

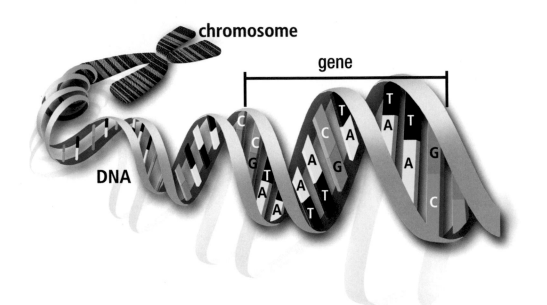

This illustration shows the highly organized structure of the genetic material within every living cell. The twisted ladder structure of the DNA molecule is called a double helix. Nitrogen bases (labeled as A, T, C, and G) create the unique code that allows every cell in the body to function properly.

should refer his or her close relatives to a carrier screening program as well.

Two blood tests are commonly used to identify carriers of the mutated hex-A gene. The first test is known as enzyme assay. This test measures the level of hex-A enzyme present in the blood. The test subject is determined to be a carrier if the amount of hex-A is significantly lower than normal. Enzyme assay tests are highly accurate and are relatively inexpensive to perform.

The second type of blood test analyzes the patient's DNA, and it is typically performed only if an enzyme assay test indicates abnormal enzyme levels. DNA screening, also known

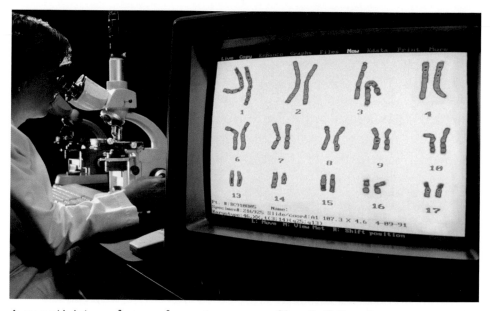

A geneticist analyzes a karyotype, a profile of all the chromosomes in one body cell of one person. Three aspects of the chromosomes are usually examined: size, banding pattern of light and dark "stripes," and centromere position. The centromere appears as a constriction, or place being pinched in, on each chromosome. By observing certain abnormalities in a karyotype, a geneticist can diagnose a person's carrier status for various genetic disorders.

as mutation analysis, studies the DNA found within the nucleus of each blood cell collected for the analysis. This DNA test looks for, and attempts to identify, specific mutations in the hex-A gene. Since 1985, when geneticists isolated the hex-A gene, almost 100 different mutations of the gene have been identified. More than 70 of those mutations have been determined to cause the infantile form of Tay-Sachs disease. Some mutations occur more frequently than others, and some are associated only with the late-onset variety of Tay-Sachs disease.

CGATTCTGAACATGATACGTACTGGTCCACTAGAACTGAACTCGAGAGGTACTAGAC

Most clinical laboratories test for the six most common mutations related to the hex-A gene. DNA testing for the purpose of carrier screening does have limitations: not all of the hex-A mutations are capable of being detected by the test, and other mutations have yet to be discovered. Often, carrier couples will use the information provided in both enzyme assay and mutation analysis to help them make decisions regarding the future of their families.

Genetic Tests for At-Risk Pregnant Women

If two carriers of the Tay-Sachs disease gene do decide to have a child, the child is considered to be at-risk. These couples have a 25 percent chance of having a baby with Tay-Sachs disease. A pregnant woman in this situation will be advised by her obstetrician to monitor her pregnancy very closely.

The two procedures described here, amniocentesis and chorionic villus sampling (CVS), are often used to monitor pregnancies when specific genetic or medical problems are suspected. In rare instances, each procedure may cause harmful side effects, and they are not routine for every pregnancy.

Amniocentesis

As a baby develops in the mother's uterus, it is cushioned and bathed in a special liquid called amniotic fluid. A procedure known as amniocentesis allows a doctor to retrieve a sample of the mother's amniotic fluid, which contain some of her baby's cells. Amniocentesis is typically performed when the mother is between fifteen and twenty weeks pregnant. To obtain a sample, a doctor will insert a thin, hollow needle through the mother's abdomen, directly into her amniotic sac.

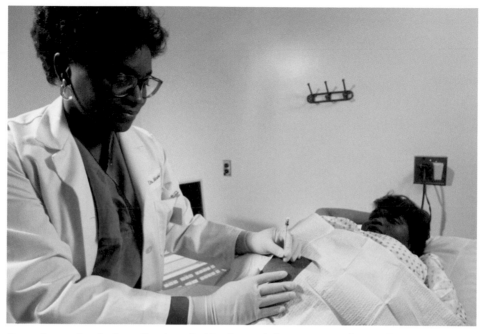

Amniocentesis is a fast, relatively painless procedure that may be performed in a doctor's office. In this photo, a physician at Baltimore University Hospital prepares her patient for amniocentesis. Once the needle has been inserted into the amniotic sac, it only takes about thirty seconds to retrieve the ounce of amniotic fluid required for genetic testing. In the days following the procedure, the developing baby produces more fluid to make up for what was lost.

The results of the amniocentesis will offer the mother and her partner crucial genetic information about their developing baby. Hundreds of genetic disorders, including Down syndrome, cystic fibrosis, sickle-cell anemia, spina bifida, and Tay-Sachs disease, can be identified using amniocentesis.

In 1971, Dr. Larry Schneck successfully made the first prenatal diagnosis of Tay-Sachs disease by performing amniocentesis and measuring the amount of hex-A enzyme

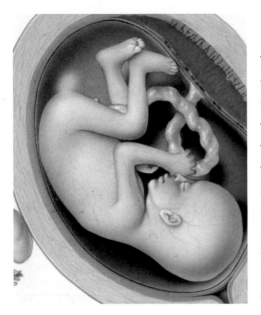

The process of a baby's development within its mother's uterus
is divided into three parts, called
trimesters, each equal to about
twelve weeks. In this illustration,
the growing fetus is in its second trimester of development. It
is during this stage of development, specifically between the
fifteenth and twentieth weeks
of pregnancy, that amniocentesis may be performed.

in the baby's cells. If the test indicated a normal amount
of hex-A, the baby would not develop Tay-Sachs disease.
If hex-A was present in significantly lower than average
quantities, the baby was clearly a carrier. Finally, if the
results indicated that hex-A was completely absent from
the amniotic fluid, the baby was diagnosed with Tay-Sachs
disease.

Chorionic Villus Sampling

Chorionic villus sampling (CVS) is a procedure that is performed in the tenth or eleventh week of pregnancy. A cell
sample is taken from the placenta, located outside the amniotic sac. The placenta is a vascular organ that develops inside
the mother's uterus. Its function is to supply food and oxygen
to the fetus through the umbilical cord. The chorionic villi are
tiny, fingerlike projections of the placenta. The cells of the
villi have the same genetic makeup as the fetus.

Many times, a doctor will obtain a sample in exactly the same way as in amniocentesis. Depending on the location of the placenta, however, a catheter may need to be inserted through the mother's vagina and into her uterus, rather than through her abdomen. The results of the procedure known as chorionic villus sampling are interpreted in exactly the same way as those for amniocentesis.

Benefits and Risks

CVS test results are reported more quickly than those of an amniocentesis. The major risk associated with both procedures is miscarriage. A miscarriage occurs when the body naturally terminates a pregnancy. The Centers for Disease Control and Prevention (CDC) reports the greatest probability of miscarriage to be 1 in 200 for amniocentesis. The risk of miscarriage with CVS is estimated by the CDC to be a bit greater. Approximately 1 in 100 CVS procedures reportedly result in miscarriage.

It should be noted that the success of either procedure depends on the skill and experience of the specialist performing it. For the carrier couples opting for either procedure, the results they receive from the amniocentesis or CVS can far outweigh any risks involved.

Genetic Counseling

Couples who are at risk for Tay-Sachs disease should consult a genetic counselor. The service provided by the counselor may vary depending on the needs of the couple. Usually, the genetic counselor educates the couple about their options for family planning. If the couple decides to have a child, they

CGATTCTGAACATGATACGTACTGGTCCACTAGAACTGAACTCGAGAGGTACTAGAC

Adoption is one alternative for couples at risk for any genetic disorder. In 2001, the United States Census Bureau reported that
there are more than 1 million adopted children in the United
States, over 2 percent of all children. A survey conducted in 1997
by the Evan B. Donaldson Adoption Institute found that six out of
ten Americans have a personal connection to adoption.

will need to understand the methods used to diagnose the
fetus. Should the tests confirm Tay-Sachs disease, the counselor will help the couple through the difficult decisions that
follow. If the couple does not wish to take the risk involved
with pregnancy, the counselor will inform them of other
options for having a baby.

One natural alternative to having their own baby would be
for the carrier couple to adopt a child. Carrier couples also have
the option to participate in various forms of assisted reproductive technology (ART). A carrier mother, for instance, may be
artificially inseminated with the sperm of a noncarrier male

A couple in Milan, Italy, seeks the guidance of a genetic counselor. If the couple wishes to embark upon any form of assisted reproduction, the counselor will explain the risks involved and the chances of conception. Genetic counselors hold graduate degrees in the areas of medical genetics and counseling. Most enter the field with previous experience or education in the fields of biology, psychology, genetics, and nursing.

donor. The carrier couple's own eggs and sperm may be used in the technology known as in vitro fertilization. Shortly after fertilization has occurred and the embryos have developed sufficiently, their DNA will be analyzed in the laboratory. Embryos that do not show evidence of hex-A mutations may then be implanted into the mother's uterus. This process is known as preimplantation genetic diagnosis (PGD). Assisted reproductive technologies involve, unfortunately, rather complex and expensive procedures. The genetic counselor helps carrier couples decide which option works best for their family.

TCGATTCTGAACATGATACGTACTGGTCCACTAGAACTGAACTCGAGAGGTACTAGA

The role of the genetic counselor takes on an extremely supportive, therapeutic role when assisting the parents of a Tay-Sachs baby. Psychological support from the genetic counselor can help parents make informed decisions about the medical care of their child and the emotional care of themselves and other family members.

Hope for the Future

Tay-Sachs disease has proven to be one of the most devastating genetic disorders in history. Due to widespread carrier screening programs initiated in the 1970s, however, the number of babies born with Tay-Sachs has dropped dramatically over the past thirty years. Finding a cure for a lysosomal storage disease such as Tay-Sachs once seemed impossible, but this may not be the case for long. Medical researchers are becoming more and more optimistic about new genetic technologies that may successfully aid in the development of a cure for Tay-Sachs disease.

Timeline

1881

Dr. Warren Tay (1843–1927) describes a patient with a red spot on the retina of his eye. This would become the first recorded case of Tay-Sachs disease.

1887

Dr. Bernard Sachs (1858–1944), a neurologist from New York City, first describes the cellular changes taking place in a Tay-Sachs patient. He also recognizes that most babies diagnosed with Tay-Sachs are of eastern European Jewish descent.

1896

Tay-Sachs disease is officially named after Dr. Warren Tay and Dr. Bernard Sachs, the two men who identified it.

1956

Amniocentesis is first used to diagnose genetic disorders by Dr. Fritz Fuchs and Dr. Povl Riis.

1969

Dr. Shintaro Okada and Dr. John O'Brien discover that hex-A is the specific enzyme missing in babies with Tay-Sachs disease.

1970

Dr. Okada and Dr. O'Brien discover that carriers of Tay-Sachs disease have reduced amounts of the enzyme hex-A in their blood cells.

(continued on following page)

(continued from previous page)

● **1971**

Dr. Larry Schneck pioneers the prenatal diagnosis of Tay-Sachs disease by measuring the amount of hex-A in the cells found in the amniotic fluid of pregnant women. Prenatal testing and intensive educational campaigns begin among members of various Jewish populations. Voluntary mass screening of adults in Jewish communities begins in order to accurately identify carriers of Tay-Sachs disease.

● **1975**

Chorionic villus sampling is successfully used for the purpose of prenatal diagnosis.

● **1985**

The hex-A gene is isolated by geneticists.

Glossary

amniocentesis A technique used to sample amniotic fluid and cells between the fifteenth and twentieth weeks of pregnancy. It is usually reserved for monitoring at-risk pregnancies when specific medical problems are suspected.

amniotic fluid The fluid present in a mother's uterus as a fetus develops.

autosome Any chromosome of the first twenty-two pairs (not the X or Y chromosome).

carrier A person who possesses only one copy of a mutated gene for a particular autosomal recessive disease. A carrier does not exhibit symptoms of the disease because his or her healthy gene overpowers the faulty gene in the pair.

chorionic villus sampling (CVS) A procedure for diagnosing prenatal genetic disorders by withdrawing a small cell sample from the placenta in the tenth week of pregnancy.

chromosome The rod-shaped strands of DNA and protein in a cell nucleus that carry the code for controlling the cell functions of an organism. There are forty-six chromosomes in human body cells and twenty-three in human sex cells (sperm or egg cells).

DNA Short for "deoxyribonucleic acid," DNA is a large molecule that stores the genetic code responsible for controlling the activity of all the cells in the body.

enzyme A type of protein in the cells responsible for bringing about a specific chemical reaction.

gene A segment of the DNA on a chromosome that contains the code for making a specific protein.

gene pool The total of all genes carried by all individuals in an interbreeding population.

lipid A fat molecule.

lysosome The structure in a cell responsible for breaking down and disposing of waste products.

mutation Any change in the genetic material of an individual that results in a disease or an abnormal gene product.

placenta A vascular organ that develops inside the uterus of most pregnant mammals to supply food and oxygen to the fetus through the umbilical cord.

stem cells Immature cells that are capable of developing into all of the different types of cells in the body.

For More Information

Canadian Association for Tay-Sachs and
    Allied Diseases (CATSAD)
569 Laural Drive
Burlington, ON L7L 5E1
Canada
(905) 634-4101
Web site: http://www.catsad.ca

Center for Jewish Genetic Diseases
Mount Sinai School of Medicine
Box 1497
One Gustave L. Levy Place
New York, NY 10029
(212) 659-6774
Web site: http://www.mssm.edu/jewish_genetics/
    index.html

National Institute of Neurological Disorders
    and Stroke (NINDS)
NIH Neurological Institute
P.O. Box 5801
Bethesda, MD 20824
(800) 352-9424
Web site: http://www.ninds.nih.gov

National Organization for Rare Disorders (NORD)
55 Kenosia Avenue
P.O. Box 1968
Danbury, CT 06813-1968
(800) 999-6673
Web site: http://www.rarediseases.org

National Tay-Sachs and Allied Diseases
    Association (NTSAD)
2001 Beacon Street, Suite 204
Boston, MA 02135
(800) 906-8723
Web site: http://www.ntsad.org

Web Sites

Due to the changing nature of Internet links, the Rosen
Publishing Group, Inc., has developed an online list of Web
sites related to the subject of this book. This site is updated
regularly. Please use this link to access the list:

http://www.rosenlinks.com/gdd/tasa

For Further Reading

Bellenir, Karen, ed. *Genetic Disorders Sourcebook* (Health Reference, Vol. 13). Detroit, MI: Omnigraphics, 1996.

Brown, Fern G. *Hereditary Diseases*. New York, NY: Franklin Watts, 1987.

Harris, Warren. *Hereditary Diseases* (Bodies in Crisis). Breckenridge, CO: Twenty-First Century Books, 1997.

ICON Health Publications. *Tay-Sachs Disease: A Medical Dictionary, Bibliography, and Annotated Research Guide to Internet Resources*. San Diego, CA: ICON Group International, 2004.

Jones, Steve, and Richard Walker. *Genes and DNA*. Boston, MA: Kingfisher, 2003.

Murphy, Wendy. *Orphan Diseases: New Hope for Rare Medical Conditions*. Brookfield, CT: The Millbrook Press, Inc., 2002.

Bibliography

Abel, Ernest L. *Jewish Genetic Disorders: A Layman's Guide.*
  Jefferson, NC: McFarland & Company, 2001.
BabyCenter Medical Advisory Board. "Prenatal Health."
  2005. Retrieved July 7, 2005 (http://www.babycenter.com/
  pregnancy/prenatalhealth).
Bellenir, Karen, ed. *Genetic Disorders Sourcebook* (Health
  Reference, Vol. 13). Detroit, MI: Omnigraphics, 1996.
Center for Jewish Genetic Diseases. "Tay-Sachs Disease."
  2005. Retrieved February 27, 2005 (http://www.mssm.edu/
  jewish_genetics/diseases).
Desnick, Robert J., and Michael M. Kaback. "Future
  Perspectives for Tay-Sachs Disease." *Advances in
  Genetics*, Vol. 44, 2001, pp. 349–356.
Fernandes Filho, Jose, MD, and Barbara Shapiro, MD. "Tay-
  Sachs Disease." *Archives of Neurology*, Vol. 61, September
  2004, pp. 1466–1468.
Gershowitz, Jayne C., ed. National Tay-Sachs and Allied
  Diseases Association, Inc. "What Every Family Should
  Know." 2003.
Mennuti, Michael T., MD. "Information About Chorionic
  Villus Sampling and Amniocentesis." University of
  Pennsylvania Health System. 1997. Retrieved July 7, 2005
  (http://obgyn.upenn.edu/genetics).

National Center for Biotechnology and Health. "Genes and Disease" and "The Nervous System." Retrieved May 9, 2005 (http://www.ncbi.nlm.nih.gov).

National Human Genome Research Institute. "Learning About Tay-Sachs Disease." Retrieved February 24, 2005 (http://www.genome.gov/10001220).

National Institutes of Health. "Clinical Trials." Retrieved April 30, 2005 (http://clinicaltrials.gov).

Woo, Joseph, MD. "A Short History of Amniocentesis, Fetoscopy, and Chorionic Villus Sampling." Retrieved July 9, 2005 (http://www.ob-ultrasound.net).

Index

A

amino acids, 14
amniocentesis, 46–48, 49
artificial insemination, 50
assisted reproductive technology
    (ART), 50–51
autosomal recessive disorder, 19–20

B

Beta-hexosaminidase (hex-A)
  function of, 16–17, 41
  measuring level of, 34, 44, 48–49
blood-brain barrier, 36

C

Canavan disease, 16
carriers
  advantage of, 28, 30
  definition of, 12
cell membrane, 17
chorionic villus sampling (CVS), 46,
    48–49

E

enzyme assay, 44
enzymes
  degradative, 15
  structure of, 14–15

F

founder effect, 31
French Canadians, 23

G

Gaucher disease, 15, 41
genetic counseling, 49–52
GM2 ganglioside, 17, 33,
    38, 41

I

in vitro fertilization, 51

J

Jews/Jewish communities, 5, 6, 11,
    28, 43
  Ashkenazi, 22–23
  history of, 24–26, 27–28
  Mizrahi, 23
  Sephardic, 23

L

lysosomal storage diseases
  definition of, 13
  examples of, 15–16
lysosomes, 13, 14, 17

M

mutations, 11–12, 15, 31, 34
　of hex-A gene, 45–46, 51

N

National Institutes of Health
　(NIH), 41
National Tay-Sachs and Allied
　Diseases Association
　(NTSAD), 34
Niemann-Pick disease, 16

O

O'Brien, John, 17
Okada, Shintaro, 17

P

preimplantation genetic diagnosis
　(PGD), 51
Punnett square, 18–19

S

Sachs, Bernard, 10–11
Sandhoff disease, 16

Schneck, Larry, 47–48
Sly syndrome, 16
statistics, 18–19, 21, 22, 23,
　28–30, 49
stem cell, 36–38, 40, 41

T

Tay, Warren, 10–11
Tay-Sachs disease
　ethnic groups commonly affected
　　by, 6, 23–24, 27–28
　infantile, 12, 22, 23, 32–33, 45
　late-onset (LOTS), 12, 33, 45
　and misdiagnosis, 34
　names for, 11, 17
　screening for, 6, 17, 23, 43
therapeutic approaches
　bone marrow transplantation, 36
　enzyme replacement therapy
　　(ERT), 35–36
　gene therapy, 38–41
　metabolic bypass therapy, 41–42
　neural stem cell therapy, 38
　substrate deprivation therapy, 41
tuberculosis, 28, 30

About the Author

Julie Walker has been teaching middle school science for over ten years. She currently resides and teaches in Sudbury, Massachusetts. Walker earned her bachelors degree in biology from Colby College in Waterville, Maine, and her masters degree in education from Lesley College in Cambridge, Massachusetts. Walker plans to incorporate everything she has learned about Tay-Sachs disease into a teaching unit in genetic disorders geared to middle school students.

Photo Credits

Cover top © Thomas Porett/Photo Researchers, Inc.; cover inset, p. 1 © www.istockphoto.com; cover background images: © www.istockphoto.com/Rafal Zdeb (front right), © www.istockphoto.com/Arnold van Rooij (front middle), © Jim Wehtie/Photodisc/PunchStock (back right), © www.istockphoto.com (back middle), © Lawrence Lawry/Photodisc/PunchStock (back left); p. 7 © Jim Dowdalls/Photo Researchers, Inc.; p. 8 © L. Wilatt/Photo Researchers, Inc.; p. 9 (left) © Mark Burnett/Science Photo Library; p. 9 (right) © Phanie/Photo Researchers, Inc.; p. 10 © Dr. Charles J. Ball/Corbis; p. 14 © Dr. Gopal Murti/Phototake; p. 16 © Alfred Pasieka/Photo Researchers, Inc.; p. 20 © Biophoto Associates/Photo Researchers, Inc.; p. 21 © 2004 Nucleus Medical Art, Inc. All rights reserved. www.nucleusinc.com; pp. 24–25 © The Art Archive/Archaeological Museum Split, Croatia/Dagli Orti; p. 27 © Corbis; p. 29 © Leonard McCombe/Time & Life Pictures/Getty Images; p. 30 © Jackie Lewin, Royal Free Hospital/Photo Researchers, Inc.; p. 35 © John Bavosi/Photo Researchers, Inc.; p. 37 © Phanie/Photo Researchers, Inc.; p. 39 © Jim Dowdalls/Photo Researchers, Inc.; p. 40 © AJPhoto/Photo Researchers, Inc.; p. 42 © 2004 Dylan James Manning Foundation For Tay-Sachs Disease; p. 44 U.S. Department of Energy Human Genome Program; p. 45 © Lester Lefkowitz/Corbis; p. 47 © Richard T. Nowitz/Corbis; p. 48 © John Karapelou, CMI/Phototake; p. 50 © Randy Santos/SuperStock; p. 51 © Mauro Fermariello/Photo Researchers, Inc.

Designer: Evelyn Horovicz; Photo Researcher: Hillary Arnold